The Child of Dreams

IRENA BRIGNULL

ILLUSTRATED BY RICHARD JONES

WALKER STUDIO

AN IMPRINT OF WALKER BOOKS LTD

High above the valley,
beyond the woods,
lived a young girl with
bluebell eyes and
hair that shone like
chestnuts.

She lived there happily
with a mother whose love
for her was stronger than
the rocks on the mountain
peak, softer than the
petals of the meadow
flowers, fuller than the
harvest moon.

Together they would laugh
and sing, gather fruit
from the trees and dig
vegetables in the garden.
They would read stories
and bake bread.

The little girl spent
most of her summer
outdoors, climbing trees
and swimming in the river.
She knew the animals and
the birds well and she saw
when they were born, how
they lived and when they
died. And she saw that each
of them had a mother
and a father.

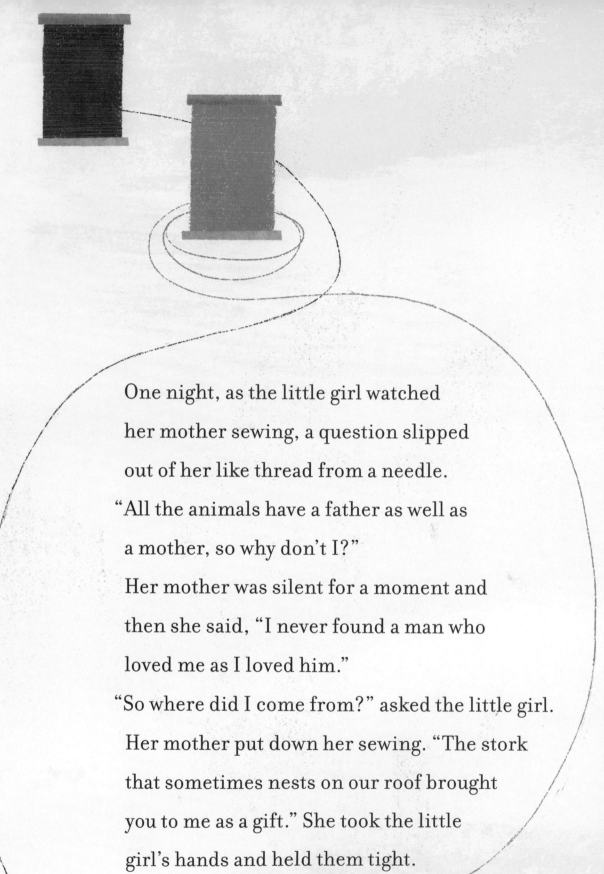

One night, as the little girl watched
her mother sewing, a question slipped
out of her like thread from a needle.
"All the animals have a father as well as
a mother, so why don't I?"
Her mother was silent for a moment and
then she said, "I never found a man who
loved me as I loved him."
"So where did I come from?" asked the little girl.
Her mother put down her sewing. "The stork
that sometimes nests on our roof brought
you to me as a gift." She took the little
girl's hands and held them tight.

The little girl felt confused. "So you didn't make me yourself?" she asked.

"I made you in my dreams," answered her mother. "I thought of you when I was a girl. I wished for you as a young woman. Then, as the years passed by, I dreamt of you every night."

The little girl let herself be hugged but, for the first time, being in her mother's arms didn't make everything feel better. Suddenly, her mother's love didn't seem quite as strong, or soft, or full.

As the days passed, the little girl didn't ask any more questions. Instead, she thought on them and they grew dark and heavy in her mind like rain within a cloud.

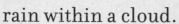

One day, when she was lying in the long grass,

the little girl saw the stork flying over her head.

She jumped to her feet and chased after her.

The stork heard her call and swooped down
to the field below, her wide, white-and-
black wings beating through the air.

"Dear stork, please tell me how you
brought me to my mother. I need to
find out where I come from."

The stork bent her long, red beak
towards the little girl and peered at her.
"Sister, the squirrels trusted me with you
when you were but a chick. I was nesting on
your roof and I knew your mother dreamt of
you at night and missed you in the days.
I knew she was the mother for you."

The little girl still felt troubled.
She packed a small bag and journeyed
into the woods until she came to a
village of squirrels.

"Squirrels, excuse me for a moment. When
I was a baby, you trusted the stork to find
me a mother. But I need to know
– where did you find me?"

The squirrels scampered and darted from the trees and gathered around her.

"Sister," they replied. "The salmon carried you up the river and asked us to take care of you. They said you were meant for land, not water."

"The salmon?" the little girl pondered. "But how did I come to be in the river?"

The squirrels shrugged their tiny shoulders. "You will have to ask them."

So the little girl travelled beyond the woods
into the fresh air and bright light of
the mountains.

Soon she came to the river, where she waited and watched for the salmon.

After a while, she saw them. Their silver scales sparkled as they leapt and danced across the rushing waters. The little girl waded into the cool river and waved her hand.

"Please, dear salmon, can I ask you but one question? I am the baby you carried upriver to the squirrels. Where did you find me?"

One of the fish swam up to her and
peered its eyes above the water's rim.
"Sister, is it you? The fox — he asked us to take
you far upstream. We took you as far as we
had the strength to carry you, for you were
meant for land, not water."

"Thank you," said the little girl.
"I would like to find this fox.
Can you tell me how to reach him?"

The little girl did as the fish advised
and followed the riverbank, uphill
and down, until she finally came to
the willow tree. There she found the
fox with fur that gleamed in the sun,
lapping the water with his tongue.

The little girl greeted the fox
cautiously, because you never can
tell with a fox how he will respond.

"Mr Fox, kind sir, perhaps
you remember a baby you once
found and gave to the salmon
to take far upstream?"

The fox sniffed the air, then looked at her.

"Of course, sister. You are that cub grown

tall and strong, I see."

The little girl smiled with relief.

"How was it that you had me in your care, dear fox?"
The fox replied, "The moon was high and the
autumn winds were stirring and I heard your
cries on the cold night air."

"I found you all alone in the dark, outside the large iron gates not far from here. I watched and waited but no one came for you. You were an orphan cub, I realized, just as I once was, so I took you away that you might find a mother."

The little girl stitched this together in her mind. She bowed her head in thanks at the fox's great help.

"You are kinder than I ever could have imagined. May I ask you for one last favour?" And she asked the fox to show her the place where he had found her.

By the large iron gates was a young boy,
sitting on the ground, staring out at the road.
The little girl looked through the gates at
the tall building behind him. She could see
many other children, big and small,
through the windows.

"Brother, what is this
place?" she asked the boy.

"It is my home," he told her,
without taking his eyes
off the road.

"What are you doing,
sitting there on the
ground all alone?"

"I am waiting. I am waiting
for someone to come for
me. Every day I wait but,
one day, I know they'll
come."

The little girl felt her mind grow foggy
with confusion.

"Do you have a mother?" the boy asked,
suddenly looking up at her.

"Yes, I do."

The boy's forehead creased. "Then why are
you here?"

"I wanted to know where I come from," answered
the little girl, suddenly less sure of her purpose.

The little boy shook his head. "And I only want
to know where I'm going."

The little girl felt the fog clear from her mind.
In its place came the picture of her mother,
searching for her high and low, calling for her
until her voice was hoarse, missing her with a love
that was stronger than mountains, softer than
petals, fuller than a harvest moon.

The little girl wished the boy goodbye and
promised to return to help him find a
mother of his own.

"There is someone out there who
is thinking of you and wishing for
you and dreaming of you, just as
my mother did for me,"
she told him.

Then she ran back past the fox with
the fur that gleamed in the sun ...

past the
salmon with
their scales
that sparkled …

past the squirrels that scampered
and darted from the trees …

and beneath the stork
with the long, red beak
and the wide, black-
and-white wings ...

back to her home,
beyond the woods,
high above the valley.

Back

to

her

mother.

Her mother cried when she saw her and held her close and kissed her hair. "My child, my child, I thought I'd lost you." Her voice shook and her arms trembled. "I'm sorry that you don't know where you come from," she whispered as she placed her hands on the little girl's face and looked into her eyes.

The little girl wiped the tears from her mother's cheeks. "Because of you, I know where I am going. You will never lose me and I will always feel found. You are my mother and I love you."

The words felt as clear as raindrops and as bright as sunshine. They lifted on the breeze and were carried away, over the trees and through the valleys to other families, far and wide …

some made by a mother and a father …

others by dreams …

some still being wished for.